Little Patriot Press

Maestro Mouse
and the Mystery of
The Missing Baton

By Peter W. Barnes and Cheryl Shaw Barnes

Cataloging-in-Publication data on file with the Library of Congress
ISBN 978-1-62157-036-3

Published in the United States by
Little Patriot Press
an imprint of Regnery Publishing, Inc.
One Massachusetts Avenue, NW
Washington, DC 20001
www.Regnery.com

Manufactured in the United States of America
10 9 8 7 6 5 4 3 2 1

Books are available in quantity for promotional or premium use.
For information on discounts and terms write to
Director of Special Sales, Regnery Publishing, Inc.,
One Massachusetts Avenue, NW, Washington, DC, 20001, or call 202-216-0600.

Distributed to the trade by:
Perseus Distribution
250 West 57th Street
New York, NY 10107

We dedicate this book to

a dear friend—our Washington, D.C., "mom"—Ambassador Esther Coopersmith, a supporter of music and the arts in our community, and a leader in improving relations among nations and in promoting goodwill and dialogue in our capital and in capitals around the world. Thank you for your friendship, support, and inspiration and for your service to our country. Bravo for our Diva of Diplomacy!

−P.W.B and C.S.B.

Acknowledgments

We wish to acknowledge the help and support of the terrific team at the Kennedy Center and the National Symphony Orchestra in the creation of this book. Also, many thanks to the supportive team at Regnery Kids including Marji Ross, Diane Lindsey Reeves, Tess Civantos, Maria Ruhl, Amanda Larsen, and Amber Colleran.

−P.W.B and C.S.B.

Little **Wolfgang** helps Maestro Mouse find his missing baton. Now find Wolfgang hidden in every illustration in the book!

The audience grows silent and the concert hall grows dim—
The stage is set, the lights go up, and someone says, "It's him!"
The master of Rachmaninoff, of Beethoven and Strauss—
A truly great conductor—now presenting Maestro Mouse!

The Maestro is incomparable, the critics all agree,
When he conducts the orchestra in any symphony!
He takes the stage most evenings in a grand old concert house,
The accoustically respected and historic Paramouse!

The orchestra's musicians are the finest in the land.
They wait for Maestro patiently, await his guiding hand,
Await not just instruction, but the Maestro's inspiration!
Quiet, now—the Maestro is so deep in concentration…

He steps on the conductor's box and turns to take a bow,
Then turns back to the orchestra, a furrow in his brow.
Then suddenly, he stops and stares—it looks like something's wrong!
He turns and shouts, "My goodness gracious! My baton is gone!"

The crowd cries out, "Oh, no! Impossible! How can it be?
With no baton, there is no tune, no notes—no symphony!"
The hall is in a panic now—the orchestra, a flurry—
When suddenly some children rush the stage. Come on now, hurry!

"Maestro Mouse," the children said, "We're here to help, you'll see!
Your baton—we'll find it fast! We'll solve this mystery!
We'll search throughout the orchestra; we'll search in every nook!
We'll search in every instrument, each cranny and each crook!"

They started in the section where the orchestra begins
In many compositions, very softly—violins!
But they didn't find it in the strings or any of the cases—
A look of disappointment came across their furry faces.

The grand piano stood nearby—they raced to check inside
To see if somewhere in it a baton might try to hide!
But no, it wasn't in the bench or in between the keys,
It wasn't in the pedals, either, or in the melodies!

It wasn't in the xylophone, the cymbals or the harp
(Though someone accidentally plucked a beautiful F Sharp).
They looked inside the French horns, too, to see what they could see.
It wasn't there—and neither was it in the timpani!

They searched the trumpets and trombones, but once again, alas,
The only thing they found in them was lots of twisted brass.
They looked inside the woodwinds next—the flutes and piccolo,
The clarinets, the big bassoon and oboes—oh, but no!

Tuba

They looked inside the tuba, too, so big and round and stout.
They turned it upside down, but no baton came tumbling out.
They ran to check the other strings, the cellos and the basses,
The violas, too, and then outside to look in other places.

They looked around the lobby and the bust of Ludwig Van
(As in the great composer, so beloved by mouse and man).
The Maestro kept up hope in the crescendo of the hunt,
As did the anxious patrons, in their seats from back to front.

But shortly, quickly, it was clear, as everyone had feared,
The baton the Maestro loved had simply disappeared!
"Come here," the grateful Maestro said, "Come all you children, now,
I thank you for your help, young friends, and please, please, take a bow."

And as they walked across the stage to follow his command,
A little mouse named Wolfgang turned and shook the Maestro's hand.
Then Wolfgang noticed something he could simply not believe:
He saw the lost baton—stuck right in the Maestro's sleeve!

Wolfgang shouted, "Maestro, look! I have found your lost baton.
It's right there, tucked in your sleeve. Now the concert can go on!"
The embarrassed Maestro mumbled, "My dear friends, I must confess:
I forgot I slipped it in there in my absentmindedness!"

"Please forgive me," he continued. And they did, of course, because
He's their one and only Maestro. They responded with applause!
"Thank you, friends," the Maestro said. "Now be quiet, if you please—
We'll begin our program shortly with Beethoven's *Ode to Cheese*."

He turned and tapped the music stand—the orchestra was ready.
He held up his baton above, so confident and steady.
Then suddenly, he pulled it down, across and in a flash—
The trumpets started pealing and the cymbals clanged and crashed!

The orchestra was wonderful, and for its presentation,
It once again received a well-deserved standing ovation!
Thanks to a great conductor, the amazing Maestro Mouse,
Who had—with genius, skill, and grace—again brought down the house!

End Notes for Parents and Teachers

The Symphony Orchestra

If one musician playing an instrument sounds nice, imagine what it sounds like when many musicians playing many different instruments come together in perfect harmony! That's what a symphony orchestra does. A group of extraordinary musicians brings their talent and instruments together as one to make beautiful music. A conductor, often called "maestro," is the leader of the orchestra. The maestro determines the musicians' seating and directs them in playing musical compositions. Highly trained in the art of conducting, he or she waves a baton to unify the musicians as they play, setting the intended rhythm, tempo, and beat of each performance. (Some conductors do not use batons, however; they conduct just with their hands.)

Orchestras can include between a few dozen musicians to more than 100. Symphony orchestras are made up of four sections:

String Section

Violins, violas, cellos, and double basses are instruments commonly found in the strings section of a symphony orchestra. String instruments use vibrating strings to make their sound. In most stringed instruments, the strings are stretched across the hollow body of a wooden instrument. Musicians make sounds by plucking the strings with their fingers or by using a bow.

Each type of stringed instrument makes different kinds of sounds or pitches depending on the length (long or short), thickness, tenseness, and density of the strings.

End Notes for Parents and Teachers

Woodwind Section

Flutes, piccolos, oboes, clarinets, bassoons, and double bassoons are woodwind instruments and are made of long, hollow tubes of wood or metal. To make sound, musicians blow air through a very thinly shaved piece of wood called a reed or across a mouthpiece. They use their fingers to open or close holes along the instrument to change the sound.

Brass Section

Horns, trumpets, trombones, and tubas are found in the brass section of an orchestra.

These instruments also use air to make sound but they are different from wind instruments in two ways: they are made of metal and they have cup-shaped mouthpieces.

To produce a note, a musician presses his or her lips to the mouthpiece and forces air out between them. This creates a vibrating column of air inside the instrument which in turn makes music. It's like making a perfect "raspberry" sound.

Percussion Section

Instruments in the percussion section make sound by being shaken or struck—instruments such as drums, cymbals, timpani (kettle drums), triangles, and xylophones.

Many orchestras also include pianos in this section. A piano is a stringed keyboard instrument with 88 notes, each making a different sound.

When you put all these instruments together, their various musical textures and tones combine to create different effects with magical, harmonious results!

End Notes for Parents and Teachers

Famous Composers

Symphony orchestras are known for playing mainly classical music. Symphonies are typically long and complex; they are unique in the way that the sounds produced by so many different instruments are layered and come together—especially when conducted by a good maestro!

Symphony orchestras are just as likely to play music composed hundreds of years ago as they are to play music written in recent years. Some of the world's most famous composers include Johann Sebastian Bach, George Frideric Handel, Wolfgang Amadeus Mozart, Ludwig Van Beethoven, and Johannes Brahms. More contemporary American composers of note include Samuel Barber, Leonard Bernstein, and John Williams. Williams is known especially for his composition and conducting of contemporary music, including "pop" concerts.

You can find out more about some of these and other notable composers at www.classicsforkids.com/composers/.

Musical Matching Game

Match the Instrument to Its Description

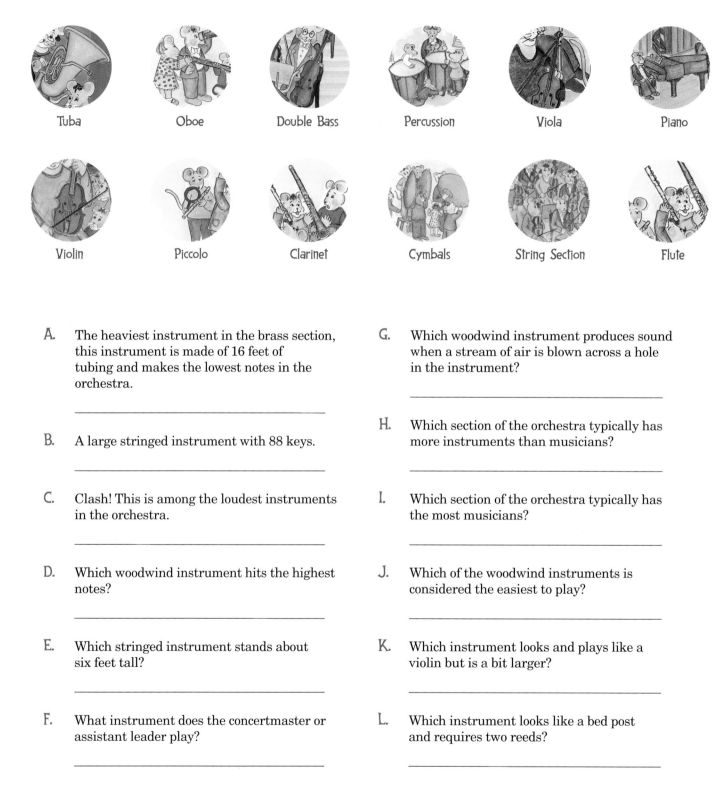

Tuba   Oboe   Double Bass   Percussion   Viola   Piano

Violin   Piccolo   Clarinet   Cymbals   String Section   Flute

A. The heaviest instrument in the brass section, this instrument is made of 16 feet of tubing and makes the lowest notes in the orchestra.

_____

B. A large stringed instrument with 88 keys.

_____

C. Clash! This is among the loudest instruments in the orchestra.

_____

D. Which woodwind instrument hits the highest notes?

_____

E. Which stringed instrument stands about six feet tall?

_____

F. What instrument does the concertmaster or assistant leader play?

_____

G. Which woodwind instrument produces sound when a stream of air is blown across a hole in the instrument?

_____

H. Which section of the orchestra typically has more instruments than musicians?

_____

I. Which section of the orchestra typically has the most musicians?

_____

J. Which of the woodwind instruments is considered the easiest to play?

_____

K. Which instrument looks and plays like a violin but is a bit larger?

_____

L. Which instrument looks like a bed post and requires two reeds?

_____

Symphonic Seating Chart

Maestros put musicians playing instruments from the same families—strings, woodwinds, brass, and percussion—together in sections to make the conducting process easier and the music more harmonious. Can you help Maestro Mouse put the correct instruments in each of the following sections?

Brass Section

A. _____

B. _____

C. _____

D. _____

Percussion Section

A. _____

B. _____

C. _____

D. _____

E. _____

F. _____

G. _____

String Section

A. _____

B. _____

C. _____

D. _____

Woodwind Section

A. _____

B. _____

C. _____

D. _____

E. _____

Triangle

Xylophone

French Horn

Violin

Piano

Harp

Trumpet

Trombone

Timpani

Flute

Cymbals

Piccolo

Clarinet

Double Bass

Bassoon

Oboe

Viola

Drums

Cello

Tuba

Size Them Up

All the instruments in the string section are made of wood and have strings. All the instruments in the brass section are made of—guess what? Brass! All the woodwind instruments are basically narrow cylinders or pipes, with holes, an opening at the bottom end, and a mouthpiece at the top. But, surprise! These days not all of them are made of wood. One of the easiest ways to tell string, woodwind, and brass instruments apart is by size. The percussion section gets a little trickier because many of these instruments share only one characteristic: they make sound when struck with the hand or a mallet. However, percussion instruments range in size from very tiny to very big.

See if you can use the word bank below to put each instrument in its section in order from smallest to biggest.

Brass Section
French Horn

Trombone

Trumpet

Tuba

1. _____

2. _____

3. _____

4. _____

String Section
Cello

Double Bass

Viola

Violin

1. _____

2. _____

3. _____

4. _____

Percussion Section
Harp

Timpani

Triangle

Piano

Xylophone

1. _____

2. _____

3. _____

4. _____

5. _____

Woodwind Section
Bassoon

Clarinet

Flute

Oboe

Piccolo

1. _____

2. _____

3. _____

4. _____

5. _____

Musical Facts and Fiction

Which of the following statements are true?

True   False   Music helps hens lay bigger eggs.

True   False   Music helps babies fall asleep.

True   False   Music helps cows give more milk.

True   False   Music helps sick people feel better.

True   False   Music helps angry people calm down.

True   False   Music helps tense people chill out and relax.

True   False   Music cheers up sad people.

True   False   Music helps plants grow.

True   False   Music helps shy elephants perform.

True   False   Music brings out creativity in people.

Answer Key If you answered true for all ten statements, you are 100% correct!

Adapted from *Ah, Music!* by Aliki (New York: HarperCollins, 2003)

Vote for Your Favorite Musical Instrument

What is the instrument that you would most like to play? Why?

_____

_____

_____

_____

_____

_____

_____

_____

_____

_____

_____

_____

_____

_____

_____

_____

Musical Resources Online

Find fun and fascinating "kid friendly" information about symphonies around the nation at the websites for the following symphonies:

Austin Symphony

Baltimore Symphony Orchestra

Boston Symphony Orchestra

Dallas Symphony Orchestra

The Kennedy Center

New York Philharmonic

San Francisco Symphony

Tucson Symphony Orchestra

Also have fun making music online at Arts Edge

http://artsedge.kennedy-center.org/educators

A Note about Maestro Mouse Illustrations

Because illustrator Cheryl Barnes lives near Washington, D.C. (in Alexandria, Virginia), she used the John F. Kennedy Center for the Performing Arts, home to the National Symphony Orchestra, as the model for many of the drawings included in this story. After all, the National Symphony celebrates all 50 states! Founded in 1931, the National Symphony Orchestra regularly participates in events of national and international importance, including performances for state occasions, presidential inaugurations, and official holiday celebrations.

For more information about the National Symphony Orchestra, visit http://www.nationalsymphony.org.

For more information about the Kennedy Center, visit http://www.kennedy-center.org.

Maestro Mouse's concert hall, the "Paramouse," is modeled after the historic Carnegie Hall in New York City. You can learn more about it here: http://www.carnegiehall.org.